Wilbur and the Wand

By **Jenny Moore**

Illustrated by **Lays Bittencourt**

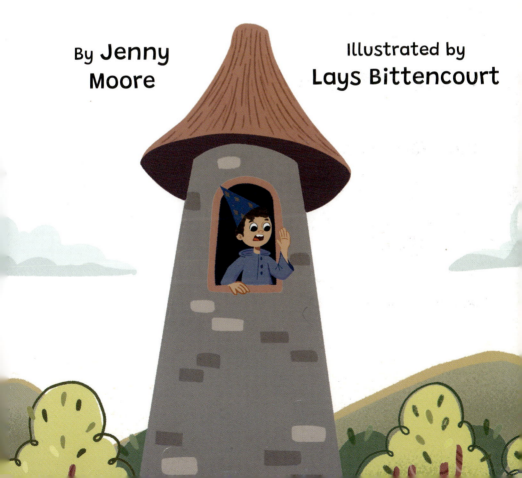

Wilbur's tower was taller than the trees...

...but there were no stairs.

Wilbur had a magic spell to fly himself up and down.

He had a magic spell
to bring his mail up
each morning too.

Ding! Dong!

Wilbur looked down from his tower.

The postman was waiting with a stack
of letters.

"You can put the letters on the ground,"
Wilbur shouted. "I will fly them up to me."

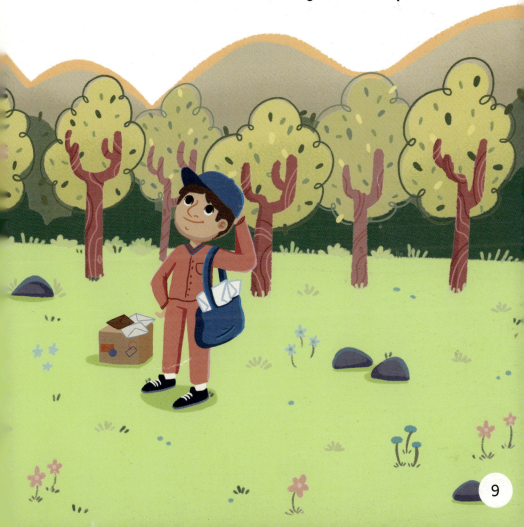

Wilbur waved his magic wand.

"Up you come,

Don't be shy.

Magic mail,

Up you fly!"

But the mail stayed on the ground.

"This wand is getting too old," moaned Wilbur.

He gave the wand one more wave.

"Up you come,

Don't be shy.

Magic mail,

Up you fly!"

The mail stayed exactly where it was.

Wilbur leaned out of the window and
waved his wand as hard as he could.

Wheee!

The wand sailed off into
the air and landed at the
bottom of the tower.

"Oh no! I need my wand to do my
magic spells! How will I get down
from my tower without it?"

"Help!" Wilbur shouted.

But the postman did not hear.

"Help!" Wilbur shouted.

But the milkman did not hear.

The painter did not hear.

The vet did not hear.

Wilbur was starting to panic.

"What if I am stuck up here forever?"

But then he spotted Wendy the window cleaner.

"Help!" Wilbur shouted and waved. "I dropped my wand and now I am stuck!"

"I can help you!" Wendy shouted up.

Wendy fetched her ladder from the van,

but Wilbur was too scared to climb down.

"I will bring your wand up to you then," said
Wendy. "I will bring your letters up too."

21

Wilbur was glad to have his wand back. "Let me make you a nice cup of tea to say thank you," he smiled.

"Now I can open my mail," said Wilbur.

He ripped open a thick brown letter.

"The new wand I sent off for!" he said

with a grin.

Wilbur tested out his new wand.

"How about,
A bite to eat?
We would like,
A tasty treat."

A huge cake appeared next to the teapot!

Wilbur cut Wendy a big slice.

Quiz

1. What does Wilbur's tower not have?
a) Stairs
b) A roof
c) Bricks

2. How does Wilbur get up and down his tower?
a) A ladder
b) Stairs
c) A magic spell

3. Why does the mail stay on the ground?
a) It's too heavy
b) Wilbur can't reach it
c) Wilbur's wand is too old

4. Who helps Wilbur?
a) The vet
b) Wendy the window cleaner
c) The milkman

5. What was in Wilbur's mail?
a) A big cake
b) A new wand
c) A magic spell

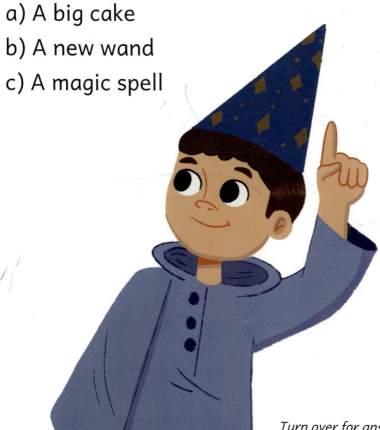

Turn over for answers

Book Bands for Guided Reading

The Institute of Education book banding system is a scale of colours that reflects the various levels of reading difficulty. The bands are assigned by taking into account the content, the language style, the layout and phonics. Word, phrase and sentence level work is also taken into consideration.

Maverick Early Readers are a bright, attractive range of books covering the pink to white bands. All of these books have been book banded for guided reading to the industry standard and edited by a leading educational consultant.

To view the whole Maverick Readers scheme, visit our website at www.maverickearlyreaders.com

Or scan the QR code above to view our scheme instantly!

Quiz Answers: 1a, 2c, 3c, 4b, 5b

Little Mouse

A Classic Fairy Tale
Illustrated by Myriam Deru

· Abbeville Kids ·

A Division of Abbeville Publishing Group

New York · London · Paris

Once upon a time, there was a young
gray mouse named Little Mouse. She lived in a
wheat field with her mother and father and bro-
thers and sisters. She was a very curious little
mouse, and she loved to look for treasures. She
found them everywhere.

Once Little Mouse found a shiny pebble under a blade of grass. Another time she found a bright blue feather behind a rock pile. Whenever Little Mouse found a treasure, her black eyes sparkled.

One warm spring day Little Mouse found a beautiful brown hazelnut under some dry leaves. It was so smooth and shiny. "This is the best treasure I have ever found," she gasped in excitement. She reached out and picked it up, but it slipped out of her paws and bounced away.

Little Mouse ran after it, but the hazelnut began
rolling down a hill. Faster and faster it went,
with Little Mouse following it. Finally, the hazelnut
bumped into a large oak tree and stopped near
a root.

Little Mouse leaned over the root and saw a round

hole. In the hole were stairs leading underground.

Suddenly the hazelnut started rolling again.
It bounced down the stairs—*tap, tap, tappity, tap.*

Without thinking about what she was doing,
Little Mouse ran down the stairs after the hazelnut.

Tap, tap, tappity, tap—down, down went the hazelnut. Little Mouse followed, until at last she reached
the bottom. Then the hazelnut rolled across to a
door. The door opened and the hazelnut rolled in.
Little Mouse hurried in after it and the door closed
behind her.

Little Mouse was in someone's home. Before her
sat a little man dressed in a red cap, a red suit, and
pointed red shoes. He was a gnome.

"You are my prisoner now," said the gnome.

"Why?" asked Little Mouse. She was very frightened.

"Because you were trying to steal my beautiful hazelnut."

"I didn't steal it," said Little Mouse. "I found it
in a field. It's mine."

"No, it's mine," said the gnome. "It rolled away
from me this morning and now it has come back."

Little Mouse looked around her, but she couldn't see the hazelnut anywhere. She wanted to go home to her family and play outside in the warm sunshine. But the gnome had just locked the door and put the key in his pocket.

"You will be my servant," he said to her. "You will make my bed, sweep my floor, and cook my soup."

Then he snickered and Little Mouse began to cry.

"And maybe, just maybe, if you work very hard, I will give you the hazelnut. It will be your reward."

And so Little Mouse became the gnome's servant.
Every day the gnome went out, locking the door
behind him and taking the key. Then Little Mouse
would make the bed, sweep the floor, and cook the
soup. She worked very hard. Every night the
gnome would return and Little Mouse would ask
for her reward.

"Not yet!" he would always say. "You haven't worked hard enough."

Spring turned into summer and summer into fall,
and still Little Mouse was the gnome's prisoner.

Then one day the gnome slept late. When he woke up, he was in a hurry to go out. As he left, he only turned the lock halfway—which meant that the door wasn't locked at all.

Little Mouse had watched him leave. She knew that at last she could escape, but she didn't want to leave without her reward. She searched everywhere

for the hazelnut. She looked in the dresser drawers. She looked in the bookcase. She looked under the rug. Where could it be?

Finally, Little Mouse saw a tiny door in the chim-
ney. She opened it and there, in a tiny cabinet, was
the beautiful brown hazelnut.

Little Mouse took the hazelnut, then carefully opened the door to the stairway and peeked out. No one
was there. Holding the hazelnut tightly, she
ran and ran—up the stairs, out the hole, around the
oak tree, and down the path to the field where she
lived. She never went back to the oak tree and she
never saw the gnome again.

How happy Little Mouse's family was to see her! She told them about being the gnome's prisoner and how hard he had made her work. "And here," she said, "is my reward." Little Mouse placed the hazelnut on the table. It clicked open, just like a jewelry box.

There inside was a very small necklace made of shiny pearls and sparkling gems. It was so beautiful! And it fit her perfectly.

Little Mouse wore her necklace often. And when she wasn't wearing it, she kept it in the hazelnut. No matter how many treasures she found—and she found many—the necklace and the hazelnut were always her favorites.

Look carefully at the objects in these pictures.

Can you find the one that went everywhere

with Little Mouse?